#8

NO FEAR

#8
NO FEAR

DEAN HUGHES

ALADDIN PAPERBACKS

First Aladdin Paperbacks edition September 1999

Copyright © 1999 by Dean Hughes

Aladdin Paperbacks
An imprint of Simon & Schuster
Children's Publishing Division
1230 Avenue of the Americas
New York, NY 10020

Also available in an Atheneum Books for Young Readers hardcover edition.

The text for this book was set in Caslon 540 Roman.

Printed and bound in the United States of America

10   9   8   7   6   5   4   3   2   1

The Library of Congress has cataloged the hardcover edition as follows:
Hughes, Dean, 1943–
No fear / by Dean Hughes.
p. cm.—(Scrappers ; #8)
Summary: Having been hit in the face by a ball during a previous game, Tracy tries to deal with her fear of its happening again as the Scrappers approach the baseball championship.
ISBN 0-689-81931-5 (hc)—ISBN 0-689-81941-2 (pbk.)
[1. Baseball—Fiction. 2. Fear—Fiction.] I. Title.
II. Series: Hughes, Dean, 1943-   Scrappers; #8.
PZ7.H87312Nn 1999   [Fic]—dc21   99-19155

CHAPTER ONE

Tracy Matlock was sitting on the grass near third base. Baseball practice had just ended, and Coach Carlton wanted to talk to the players before they left. Tracy's eye was still swollen from a blow she had taken in the last game, when a ground ball had taken a bad hop and caught her under her left eye. The deep purple shiner was already shading toward green around the edges, and she had a scrape across her cheekbone.

Cindy Jones was sitting on one side of Tracy and Gloria Gibbs on the other. The three had been talking about their next game, against the Stingrays. Cindy finally asked the question that Tracy knew was coming. "So . . . Tracy . . . how was it today? Did the ground balls scare you a little?"

"Naw," Tracy said, trying to sound relaxed.

"I've been playing this game a long time. I'm not going to let one little poke in the eye worry me."

But Tracy's voice had sounded tight—even to herself. She felt the silence on both sides of her. Finally, Gloria said, "Tracy's pretty tough—for a rich girl." She laughed and threw an elbow into Tracy's shoulder.

That didn't help at all. The truth was, Gloria thought Tracy was pretty soft. And Tracy was also getting tired of all the cracks about being rich. When the two had been younger, things like that never seemed to matter, but lately Gloria had started to make a big deal out of Tracy living in Mountain Oaks, the nicest subdivision in town.

Still, Tracy let Gloria's little dig go by. "Hey, I handled everything that came to me today," she said.

That should have been the end of it, but Gloria had to say, "Yeah, well, the coach took it easy on you. He kept hitting those nice little bouncers your way."

Robbie Marquez and Wilson Love were sitting together, and they both turned around.

"No, he didn't," Wilson said. "You'll be fine, Trace. Just go after the ball like you always do."

But Tracy wondered what he really thought. Wilson must have seen her flinch a few times when the ball was hit right at her.

The coach walked over to the kids. "Good workout today," he said. "I really feel like we're hitting a peak, playing our best ball of the season."

"Too bad it's too late," Trent Lubak mumbled.

Everyone knew what Trent meant. The Scrappers were one game behind the Mustangs with two games to go. Someone would have to beat the Mustangs, or the season would be over for the Scrappers.

"Maybe the Mustangs will lose again tomorrow," Robbie said. "They haven't been hitting that well lately."

"It's hard to say," Coach Carlton said. "What we need to do is play smart, the way we did against the Pit Bulls the other day. If we win both our games, who knows? Maybe the Mustangs will lose one, and we'll get another chance."

"If we end up tied at the end of the season, what exactly will happen?" Cindy asked.

"First we'd have to play the Mustangs for the second-half championship. Then, if we beat them, we'd play them again—for the league championship. Now *that* would be a lot of fun."

Tracy wasn't so sure. It was hard to imagine that the Scrappers could beat the Mustangs twice. But that wasn't the only thing bothering her. It did scare her to think of taking another hard shot in the face. The coach really *hadn't* hit any hard ones to her; Gloria was right about that. Tracy wasn't sure what she would do the first time a real screamer came her way.

The coach talked to the kids about remembering what they had learned and about playing as a team. When he finished, all the players got up from the grass. Tracy had left her street shoes in her athletic bag, so she walked over to the dugout to get them. But just as she was leaving the dugout, Martin Epting came up to her. "Hey, you did fine for the first time back," he said.

Tracy stopped. "What's that supposed to mean?"

"Nothing. Just what I said."

"I thought I did fine, period."

"You did. You just turned your head a little on a couple of those ground balls—but who wouldn't?"

"Hey, maybe *you* would. But I didn't. You must be seeing things."

"Okay. Okay." Martin turned so red that when he ducked his head Tracy could see his scalp blushing through his dark hair. She wished that she hadn't been so rough on him. He was actually a nice guy. But where did he get off, saying something like that? Okay, so maybe he was right. He still didn't have to say it.

The next evening Tracy's parents gave her a ride to the game. For the first time ever, her friends Heather, Maria, and Kim came along. The girls all lived near Tracy in Mountain Oaks. The houses were quite big, but they weren't mansions, the way Gloria claimed. Tracy's father was a doctor, but he was a family physician, not some wealthy specialist. He was the kind of guy who helped a lot of people who couldn't afford to pay him. That was one of the reasons Tracy hated it when Gloria called her family rich—her parents never acted like they were big shots, and Gloria knew that.

Heather and Kim had moved into Tracy's

neighborhood only the year before, but Tracy had known Maria most of her life. None of the girls were into sports at all, and Tracy wasn't really all that close to any of them. She'd been a little surprised recently when she discovered she actually enjoyed hanging out with them sometimes. But for some reason Tracy liked keeping her neighborhood friends and her baseball friends apart.

It had been her mom who had invited the girls to today's game. The fact was, Mrs. Matlock was not all that excited about Tracy playing ball—and getting hurt again. She really wanted Tracy to develop some other interests. Her mom was never pushy about it, but Tracy knew what she hoped: that Tracy would hang around more with the girls in the neighborhood, and less with Gloria.

There was no hiding it. Mrs. Matlock didn't like Gloria very much. She thought the girl was too loud, too ready for a fight. Tracy kept telling her that Gloria was changing, and Mrs. Matlock had to grant that, but she would always tell Tracy, "Honey, the only thing that girl cares about is sports. I don't want you to be that one-dimensional."

Tracy didn't exactly argue the point. She did

think Gloria was too much of a sports nut. But bringing Maria and the other girls to the game had been a mistake. Gloria thought Maria was the snootiest "rich girl" in town, and Maria didn't know anything about baseball.

"Good luck," Heather said, as Tracy headed for the diamond.

"Don't worry," Maria said. "Tracy's an *incredible* player. Tonight she's playing against Elise Harris and Elvin Badger—some kids like that. That should be no problem."

"Look, I'm not *that* good," Tracy said. "And the Stingrays have this guy named Bennett on their team. Everyone calls him 'Bullet.' He's a tough pitcher. We've beaten him before, but—"

"Oh, don't worry. You'll win. And we can celebrate later at my house when we watch that video I rented." Maria was a small girl with curly black hair. To Tracy, she seemed a little too dressed up, in nice shorts and a pretty red top— but then, Maria always wore nice clothes. It was also a little annoying that she seemed so sure of who would win. The girl hadn't been to a game all season.

As Tracy walked to the dugout, Gloria came out to meet her. Of course, she had to say,

"What's going on? Why did you bring the rich crowd with you?"

"I didn't. My mom invited them."

"I don't know why they came. They won't even know what's going on."

"That's probably true," Tracy said. She tried to take on Gloria's disgusted tone. She really wanted to separate herself from the girls—and not take a teasing about them all evening.

The opportunity was too good for Gloria to pass up, however. "You might as well get used to it," she said. "You'll probably have to hang around with rich people all your life. That's one thing *I* don't have to worry about."

Tracy didn't want this tonight. She walked away. Then she tried to get her mind on the game and forget about everything else. What she had to do tonight was handle every ground ball that came her way—and show her teammates that she wasn't scared.

Maybe she had to show herself, too.

She was actually happy when the first batter for the Stingrays, Petey Peterson, knocked a ground ball right at her. It wasn't hit hard, but it was a good chance to get the jitters behind her. She charged the ball smoothly, watched it come up on a nice hop, fielded it cleanly with both hands, and then set her feet before she tossed the ball to Adam Pfitzer at first.

It was "by the book" all the way, and Tracy was relieved.

She got a cheer from the Scrappers' fans, and she heard her parents and the three girls pour it on just a little too thick. "You're the *best*, Trace," she heard Maria shout.

Tracy knew better than to look at Gloria. But she heard Gloria imitate the high-pitched voice: "You're the best, Trace."

Tracy walked toward Gloria, blocked the view of her mouth with her glove, and pretended she was giving Gloria a signal. But actually, she said, "Shut up, dirt ball."

Gloria put her own glove up and said, "Say that again and I'll make your whole face black and blue."

The two shared a laugh, and Tracy felt a lot more relaxed. She walked back to her position.

Ollie Allman, who was pitching tonight, stayed in his own world during a game, and that seemed to work for him. Tracy could hear him mumbling, but she couldn't pick up the words. He had improved his control all season, and

lately he was really throwing well. He threw
Elise Harris a beautiful pitch on the inside of
the plate, down at the knees.

Elise was a good hitter, but she went after
the pitch and rolled it in the dirt in front of the
plate. Adam broke from first base toward the
plate, but the ball died quickly. It was Wilson
who fielded it. Tracy had seen all that coming,
and she ran hard for first. She was there in
plenty of time. Adam ducked down, and Wilson
fired a strike to Tracy.

Two away.

"That's it, Tracy," Coach Carlton yelled.
"That's being right where you need to be."

Tracy was suddenly very glad to be out on
the baseball field. A play like that, with everyone working together, was what made the game
great.

Michael Reynolds, the Stingrays' star player,
was up next. He loved to go through a routine
before he stepped into the box. He knocked the
dirt from his shoes, straightened his wristbands,
took off his hat and put it back on, just right.

"Just get up there and bat!" Gloria shouted
at him.

He nodded to her, as if to say, "Don't worry, I will."

Then he took a pitch for a strike that he thought was outside. He stepped out and whined about it to the ump. Gloria was all over him again.

When he finally got ready, Ollie put another pitch in the same spot, and this time Reynolds went after it. But he didn't get it all. He hit a gentle fly to center, and Thurlow Coates trotted to his left a few steps and hauled it in.

Good start. Three up, three down.

The Scrappers ran off the field, and then Jeremy Lim got a bat and walked toward the plate. As he did, Bennett went out of his way to walk over to him. The two exchanged a few words, and then Bennett walked onto the mound and took his warm-up pitches.

Jeremy took a pitch that looked low to Tracy, but the umpire called it a strike. Then, on the next pitch, Jeremy poked the ball to center field. But he hit it a little too hard, and it stayed up. Jimmy Saunders, the center fielder, charged the ball and took it for the first out.

Jeremy ran back to the dugout as Robbie

walked to the plate. "What was Bennett telling you?" Tracy asked Jeremy.

"He told me, 'Don't even think about winning tonight. I'm blowing you guys away.'"

"What did you tell him?"

"Nothing. I just said, 'We'll see about that.' And then he said, 'I'd stay loose at the plate if I were you—and you can tell your whole team that.'"

"What's that supposed to mean?" Chad Corrigan asked.

"Don't be stupid," Gloria told Chad. "He's saying he'll throw at us. And I'm saying, just try, Bennett. Just try."

But the threat made Tracy nervous.

CHAPTER TWO

Robbie was up, and he hadn't heard Bennett's warning. He looked confident as he stepped to the plate. He swung his bat a couple of times and then got set.

The first pitch was right at Robbie. He dropped like he had been shot. For a moment Tracy thought the ball had hit him, but Robbie had managed to get down quickly, and the ball had sailed over him. Badger, the catcher, had to jump sideways to block the ball. He didn't catch it, but he knocked it down.

"That was on purpose!" Adam shouted to the ump. "He said he was going to do it."

But the umpire didn't pay any attention.

Coach Carlton walked over to the dugout. "Did that boy say something about throwing at our players?" he asked.

"Yeah," Jeremy said. "He told me we all better stay loose at the plate."

"Well . . . maybe that's not what he meant," the coach said. "Let's give him the benefit of the doubt." He walked back to the coach's box.

Bennett's next pitch was a curve. The ball broke outside, and Robbie watched it go by for a ball.

Then Bennett came with a fastball away, and Robbie reached for it and drove it hard down the right field line. It settled in for a base hit, and John Jefferson, the big right fielder, didn't hurry to get over to it. Robbie saw that and took off for second. Jefferson got serious at that point, and he made a strong throw, but Robbie slid in well ahead of the tag.

Bennett looked mad enough to chew up the pitching rubber. He waited to get the ball back, and then he socked it into his glove a couple of times before he took his position on the mound.

Gloria was up next. She stood outside the batter's box and yelled, "Hey, Bennett, you didn't scare Robbie. And you don't scare me."

"That's enough," Tracy heard the umpire tell Gloria. But she reached down and grabbed some dirt, which she rubbed into her hands. Then she wiped her hands on her shirt, which was already dirty.

Bennett nodded to the catcher's signal, and then he let go with a harpoon shot—right at Gloria's head. Gloria twisted and ducked out of the way. She had to put one hand down to catch her balance, but she came up ready to fight. She ran about four steps toward Bennett and then stopped.

For a moment, she stared at Bennett. Then she spun around and yelled to the ump, "He threw at my head. You saw it."

The umpire walked out in front of the plate. "That's two inside ones," he told Bennett. "You better not be throwing at these batters."

"The ball got away from me, that's all," Bennett said.

Tracy was amazed that Gloria had held herself back, that she had stopped halfway to the mound. The old Gloria wouldn't have done that.

Coach Carlton was walking to the plate. "The boy made some threats before the game," he told the umpire. "We can't have that kind of stuff going on out here."

"I didn't threaten nobody," Bennett said. He

walked off the mound toward the plate. "That's just a big lie."

The umpire turned on Bennett. "You throw one more pitch like that, and I'll have you suspended for the rest of the season. Do you hear me?"

"Yeah. But what if I can't help it? Sometimes I don't have very good control." He glanced at Gloria, and Tracy thought she saw a hint of a smile.

"Just don't be wild inside, not if you want to keep playing."

"That's not fair," Bennett mumbled, and he turned and walked back to the mound. But he didn't throw another pitch inside.

Gloria wasn't frightened, she was too mad. She clearly wanted to belt one out of the park, and she was swinging wildly. She struck out swinging, and that was something she didn't do very often.

Thurlow wasn't one to get scared—or mad—but he did get a little too eager sometimes. When Bennett fed him a high fastball, Thurlow should have let it go by. But he went up after it and sent a high fly ball to left field. It was an easy out, and the side was retired.

So the Scrappers headed for the field, but Tracy didn't like the feeling in the park. All the Stingrays were mouthing off as they ran to their dugout. Bennett walked as far as the first base line, and then he looked back at Ollie. "Hey, weird boy," he said. "Talk to yourself all you want. You aren't going to beat us today."

"Shut your mouth," Wilson yelled at Bennett. "Get off the field."

The umpire told both of them to be quiet, and Coach Carlton yelled, "Wilson, no more of that. Just don't pay any attention to him."

Tracy hated all this. She looked up at the bleachers and wondered what the girls from her neighborhood thought. Baseball was a great game, but a guy like Bennett could make it seem ugly. She didn't know why some guys had to act like that. "Come on, Ollie," she yelled. "Just chuck it in there. Forget all that stuff."

Ollie didn't seem to hear her. But then, he didn't seem to hear anyone. He was searching for his zone again, talking to himself. When

Elvin Badger stepped to the plate, Ollie threw him a good fastball on the outside edge of the plate. Elvin chased it and fouled the ball off.

But Ollie's next pitch didn't have much on it. It didn't come hard, but it was inside, and Badger had to jump out of the way. Immediately, the Stingrays' coach ran out of his dugout. "What do you call that, ump? Now who's throwing at the batters?"

Wilson stood up and spun around. "No way," he said. "He was trying to throw a curve. It didn't break for him."

The umpire looked over at the Stingrays' coach. "That ball had nothing on it," he said. "I don't think he was trying to hit anyone."

"It goes both ways, ump. If you're going to warn my kid, warn this boy, too."

The umpire looked out at Ollie. "We're not going to let anything get started here," he said. "Do you understand that?"

Ollie said something, but not loud enough for anyone to hear. Maybe he was responding, maybe mumbling, but he didn't seem mad. In fact, he was the only player out there who didn't appear upset.

Ollie threw a good fastball, down in the strike zone. Badger went after it and hit the ball hard on the ground. It was bouncing to Tracy's left, and she darted after it. She stabbed the ball on a short hop, and her momentum carried her forward. She stumbled, but then she did a complete three-sixty to get herself stopped.

She finally got set and tossed the ball to Adam just as Badger stretched to tag the base. It was a close play, but the umpire shouted, "Out!"

Tracy had ended up close to the first base line. Badger, as he overran the bag, charged past her. But as he did so, he veered inside the line enough to hit her with his shoulder and spin her around.

Tracy didn't go down, and she wasn't hurt, but she was furious. She turned and faced Badger, who was now walking toward her. "Just try that again!" she shouted at him. "I'll be ready for you next time."

Badger laughed. "Hey, you got in my way," he said. "Do it again and I'll knock you into right field."

But now the umpire was yelling at them. "Hey, you two, that's enough."

Tracy spun around. "He tried to knock me down," she yelled.

"She got in my way," Badger said, but he was still laughing.

"Both of you, stop right now. This is my last warning." The umpire turned around. "Coaches, I'm calling both teams off the field for a couple of minutes. Talk to your players and get them under control. One more incident, and I'm calling this game off. And if I do, both teams will take a loss on their records."

Tracy had calmed down, but now she was embarrassed. In the car, on the way to the game, she had tried to convince Maria, Heather, and Kim that baseball was a great game, and now they were seeing something that looked more like tag-team wrestling. She walked across the diamond toward the coach.

"Now listen," Coach Carlton told the players. "The Stingrays are not as good as you kids are, so they're trying everything they can to get you upset. If you lose your cool, all you're doing is giving them what they want."

"Badger tried to run me down," Tracy said. "The ump didn't see it, but he—"

"I saw it," Coach said. "There's no question about it. That's what he did. But their season is over. They've got nothing to lose. If we get into another beef with them and get this game cancelled, we're going to lose the last chance we have for the championship. So I don't care what those kids do or say from this point on, we're going to look and act like real players—like the champions we are. Do you hear me?"

The players all said they did, and Thurlow said, confidently, "Let's just score runs. That'll shut them up."

"That's right," Coach Carlton said. "Let's talk it up. But don't say one word to the Stingrays—or anything about them. Just back up your own players."

So the team ran back onto the field shouting support to Ollie. The Stingrays weren't saying much of anything. Tracy figured they were being careful, but she doubted they had changed their attitudes.

John Jefferson came up. He gave Ollie a hard look, his eyes still full of anger. But he took some hard cuts and never touched the ball. He struck out.

Then Bennett stepped to the plate. He nodded at Ollie, as if to say, "You're mine."

Ollie threw a change-up on the first pitch, and clearly, Bennett was looking for heat. He swung way out in front of the pitch and only managed to nub the ball off the end of his bat.

The ball rolled into the dirt in front of the plate, and Wilson was on it immediately. Bennett didn't even bother to run. Wilson picked up the ball, tagged Bennett, and the top of the inning was over.

From the dugout, the Stingrays' coach was screaming at Bennett, chewing him out for not running. Tracy was glad she wasn't on that team, with that coach. But she was still embarrassed that she had let Badger get to her.

CHAPTER THREE

The Stingrays were being a little more careful now, but they were still quietly throwing little insults at the Scrappers. They were also ragging on one another. The Scrappers were doing a good job of staying away from all that, and even Gloria wasn't returning the smack talk.

In the bottom of the second inning, Tracy came up with Wilson and Trent on base. She wanted to show her friends what she could do, but she was a little nervous about Bennett's fastball. The idea of taking a fastball in the head was frightening, and it was hard not to think about it.

Tracy didn't back away, however. She stayed in there and took her swings. But she struck out on a pitch that *pounded* into Badger's glove. As she turned to walk away, she heard Badger laugh. It was all she could do not to explode at him again. Instead, she walked away without showing him that she had heard. And then Adam also struck out, and Ollie grounded out to the third baseman.

Ollie finally gave up a scratch hit in the third inning, but then he put the Stingrays away again; so going into the bottom of the inning, there was still no score in the game. Things didn't look any better when Jeremy and Robbie both hit fly balls for outs. But Gloria hung tough against Bennett and punched an outside pitch to the opposite field. It dropped in front of the right fielder for a single.

Thurlow stepped to the plate. The first pitch was high. Tracy saw Thurlow start his swing and then hold up. He was going to play it smarter this time, not go chasing after bad pitches.

He took another pitch, still high, and then Bennett got one in Thurlow's power zone. Thurlow's stroke was so quick that when the ball shot toward left, Tracy was sure it would be caught. But it was a line shot that was still rising when it passed over the fence.

Home run!

Thurlow had come through, and the Scrappers were on top 2 to 0. When Tracy saw how frustrated and angry Bennett was, she fully expected him to fall apart. He did give up a single to Wilson, but he blew Trent away, and the inning was over.

Tracy had been waiting on deck and hoping for her chance to keep a big inning going, but now she grabbed her glove and headed back to the field.

Elise Harris was up first for the Stingrays in the fourth. She got caught off guard by Ollie's curveball. She stabbed at the ball and sent it rolling to the right side. Tracy broke to her left, Adam to his right. Adam made the stop, and Ollie hustled over to cover first.

It was a close play, but Adam got the ball to Ollie, and Ollie's foot hit the bag just in time.

It was nicely done, the kind of play that took some good timing, good team play. The crowd gave the Scrappers a nice hand, and Coach yelled, "That's the way we do it. Good job." Tracy felt herself relaxing a little more.

Reynolds stepped in. He swung at the first

pitch and shot a hard grounder foul, down the third base line. He had really gotten around on Ollie's fastball.

Tracy saw Wilson signal for a change-up. It was a good idea. She shifted a couple of steps to her right. She expected Reynolds to swing way too soon. But he seemed to be looking for an off-speed throw. He waited on the pitch, and then he hammered it deep to left. The ball was hit high, and Tracy thought Trent might have a chance to catch it. But it carried well, and it dropped over the fence.

So the lead was cut in half: 2 to 1.

This was simply not going to be easy. Badger was coming up, and by the look on his face, he wanted to leave the yard with another one and get the game tied.

Ollie was looking up at Mount Timpanogos. Tracy heard him say to himself, "Badger doesn't worry me. He'll swing at anything. Just feed him stuff outside."

Tracy figured she'd better shift back a little to her left, if that's how Ollie was going to pitch him. She knew one step could make all the difference on a hard-hit ball.

Ollie got the first pitch outside, but way outside, and Badger didn't swing. The next pitch was close, and Badger took a cut and missed.

Now Wilson moved the target to the inside edge, and Ollie tried to bust him in tight. The pitch was close, barely inside, but Badger spun away and shouted to the umpire, "He's throwing at me again."

Tracy heard the umpire say, "That pitch was almost in the strike zone."

Badger seemed to know better than to complain much more. He stepped back to the plate. This time Ollie went back outside, and Badger took another big swing—and connected. He sent a hard shot on the ground, straight at Tracy.

Tracy had only a moment to react. She stayed low and got her glove down, but the ball skipped high and bounced off the heel of her glove. She had stayed in front of the ball, and it dropped on the ground where she could grab it. She picked it up and made an easy throw to Adam for the out.

It was actually a routine play. She had done everything right. Almost everything.

All the Scrappers were yelling, "Way to go,

Trace. Good job." But Tracy looked over at Gloria, and Gloria looked troubled. Tracy immediately looked away. She socked her fist into her glove and walked back to her position. She didn't want to admit it to herself, but she knew the truth. At the last instant, as the ball had come up on her, she had looked away, turned her head to avoid taking another blow in the face.

Maybe she wouldn't have fielded the ball cleanly anyway. But she knew she hadn't looked the ball into her glove. Had she been afraid? Was she going to be afraid from now on?

Jefferson was up. She needed to think about that. He was very slow, so she could cheat back just a little. It gave her more time to field a ground ball and still throw him out. He could hit the ball hard, and it helped to have a little more room to work. Or was she moving back because she was scared?

"Hit it right here, Jefferson," Tracy chanted. "I got your number."

But she knew she was just trying to convince herself of that. She was hoping he would hit it somewhere else, that she wouldn't have to handle another tough play right now.

As it turned out, Jefferson didn't hit the ball anywhere. Ollie kept him off balance. He pitched the ball in and out, changed speeds, and finally struck Jefferson out on a mean fastball at the knees and on the outer edge.

So the Scrappers still had their lead, and Tracy was going to get a chance to make something happen on offense. As she ran off the field, she shouted, "All right. Let's get some runs now."

But she didn't look at Gloria. She ran to the bat rack and found the bat she always used. She walked away from the other players and took some swings. She was going to handle ol' Bullet this time.

But as she walked to the plate, she felt the butterflies in her stomach—worse than she remembered in a long time. Was it because her friends from her neighborhood were there? Or was it because the game meant so much?

Or was it Bennett's fastball?

She purposefully set up a little closer to the plate than usual. She wanted Bennett to see that she was right there, ready to go after him.

But when Bennett released his first pitch,

she saw the ball boring through the air straight at her head. She dropped on the ground to get out of the way.

As she was falling, she knew that the pitch hadn't been that close after all.

"Ball one!" the umpire said. At least it hadn't been a strike.

Badger was laughing again. He didn't say a word, but she knew what he was thinking—that she was afraid of Bennett.

She dug in again and this time set herself. If he hit her in the forehead, she wasn't going to back away. But this pitch was over the plate, and Tracy didn't trigger. She felt frozen in her stance, and she didn't know why.

She couldn't do that again. But the next pitch was low, and she went after it anyway. She fouled it into the dirt.

"Come on, Tracy. Concentrate," the coach was yelling. "Stroke this one."

But Bennett threw another inside pitch.

At least Tracy didn't hit the dirt. She took a hard swing. But she felt herself stepping away as she swung. She missed the ball and struck out.

Badger was still laughing.

"Shut up," Tracy told him as she walked

away. And then she took off her batting helmet and tossed it toward the bat rack. When she walked into the dugout, she sat down at the closest end, so she wouldn't have to walk past everyone.

Gloria got up, came over to her, and sat down. "What's going on?" she asked.

"Nothing."

"Don't give me that. You're acting like little Miss Prissy out there."

"Shut up."

"You took a dive, and the ball was almost over the plate. You're thinking more about your cute little face than you are about our game."

"Shut up, Gloria. You don't know what it's like." The words came out before she had had time to think. She had admitted more than she wanted to.

"What are you talking about? You think I've never been hit by a ground ball?"

"Not like I got hit."

"Oh, come on. That's stuff your mom is feeding you." Gloria changed her voice to a high-pitched, simpering tone. "You won't ever be prom queen, my little sweety, if you get bumps all over your face."

"Just shut up. I can handle anything you can."

"Well, then, prove it." Gloria got up and walked back to where she had been sitting before, next to Thurlow and Wilson.

Tracy was furious. She vowed to herself that she wouldn't mess up again. But Gloria was wrong about one thing. Tracy wasn't afraid of getting another black eye just because it would look bad. She was simply scared of the ball. She had been telling herself all the right things, but she couldn't seem to control her reaction, and that reaction was to protect herself from getting hit in the face again.

CHAPTER FOUR

The Scrappers didn't score in the fourth inning, and neither team scored in the fifth. The score was still 2 to 1, and Ollie was getting the job done on the mound. But a one-run lead was very little to hang on to.

At the start of the sixth, Coach Carlton put Cindy in the game for Tracy. Tracy was relieved, in a way, but she had wanted to prove something, and she hadn't had the chance. She had made a couple of decent fielding plays early in the game—and took care of an easy grounder in the fifth—but that was about it.

Martin was also going in to play right field for Jeremy, and Chad was replacing Adam. All that worried Tracy. She wondered whether the lead could hold with those kids in the game. Some teams, in tight games, didn't bother to substitute. It was Coach Carlton's rule to do so, not a league rule. Tracy knew the three subs had improved a great deal, but in a tight spot . . . who could say?

Tracy glanced at her friends, up in the crowd. As the game had gone on, the three had turned more and more toward one another. Tracy doubted they even knew what the score was. Obviously, they were talking about something other than the game: school or boys or clothes. Tracy really didn't care.

The first batter in the sixth was a kid named Walters, the ninth batter and probably the worst player in the Stingrays' lineup. Ollie blitzed him with a couple of fastballs, and the kid didn't move. Just when it seemed that Ollie would put him away, Walters started to swing at a pitch inside and then held up. The ball hit his bat, and it bounced onto the grass down the third base line.

Wilson was after the ball quickly, but it rolled far enough that it turned into a pretty good bunt. Still, Wilson had it in plenty of time. He turned and threw hard. It was not a terrible throw, but low. Chad seemed to have it for a moment, and then it dropped on the grass. He quickly grabbed it with his bare hand, but Walters, slow as he was, had crossed the bag.

Tracy hated to see something like that happen. Walters had been a sure out, and now he was on, and the top of the order was coming up. But Petey hit a nice ground ball right to Cindy, and it came up perfectly for her. She made the stop, and all she had to do was flip the ball to second to get the lead runner. Gloria raced to the bag and was ready, but Cindy threw too hard and too wide. Gloria made a fantastic catch, but the throw pulled her off the bag. Walters was safe again.

Tracy couldn't believe this. She felt sick. Runners were at first and second now, and no one was out. She really believed that if she had been out there, she would have made a good throw, and Gloria would have turned the double play.

But now Elise Harris, a first-rate hitter with great bat control, was up there with the tying run in scoring position.

Ollie took his time. He was talking softly, even looking at the ball at times, as though he were trying to tell it what to do. His first pitch had some fire behind it. Elise tried to poke it to the right side, but she swung late and fouled it into the crowd.

The Stingrays had really come to life now. Bennett shouted at Ollie, "Throw another one like that, and Elly will lose it for you."

"There's no way he'll do that," Badger yelled. "Ollie can't throw two strikes in a row."

Earlier in the season that might have been true, but now Ollie threw another good pitch that looked like a strike to Tracy. The umpire called it a ball, but Wilson shook his head as he came up out of his stance. "Looked good to me," he yelled to Ollie.

Ollie nodded. He caught the return throw, and then he talked to the ball again—which brought on all the more abuse from the Stingrays. He didn't pay any attention. He fired another hard fastball. But this time Elise stroked it. She drove the ball toward Martin in right field. Tracy's breath caught.

Martin charged the ball, but it was sinking fast. It looked like a sure base hit. But Martin did something surprising. He didn't slow down to take the ball on the first bounce. Instead, he reached down and grabbed for it, on the fly, just above the grass.

Tracy couldn't tell. Had he caught it or not? The runners were stuck halfway between bases, wondering the same thing. Then the Stingrays' coach bellowed, "Base hit! Go!"

At the same moment, Martin raised his glove and showed that he had caught the ball.

The umpire in the field hollered, *"Out!"*

Cindy was on her base at second, and Gloria was covering third for Robbie. Cindy shouted, "Second base!" Martin turned and made a rather weak, looping throw to second.

Petey had listened to his coach and not the umpire. He was sliding into second. Meanwhile, Walters had gotten the message from the third base coach. He had reversed himself and was heading for the same base. Both runners converged on second, with Cindy standing in the middle.

She caught the ball and tagged the base, just as Walters was sliding back to the bag.

"Out!" the umpire yelled again.

Then she reached down and tagged Petey, who was still on the ground.

"Out!"

Tracy had lost track. She tried to figure out what had happened. And then she realized. The Scrappers had just pulled off a triple play!

Martin and Cindy had come through. Big-time!

The score was still 2 to 1, and the Scrappers only had to survive one more inning.

But the Stingrays weren't buying it. The coach ran onto the field, shouting, "That kid in right didn't catch that ball. He trapped it against the ground. What are you trying to pull?"

Mr. Klein, the Stingrays' coach, was a little guy with a big, bushy mustache and a high voice. He was always noisy during the games, but Tracy had never seen him as upset as he was now. His face was red, and his voice was pinching off into squeaks. The umpire turned his back and walked away from the man.

But that only brought on a wilder scream. "What's going on here? Can't you see? Is that your problem?"

Suddenly the umpire spun around. "Get off this field right now or I'll call this game, and your kids will have to forfeit."

"Fine. You do that. And I'll take this up with the Recreation Department. I think there's something going on here."

"That's it. This game is—"

"No. Wait a minute." Coach Carlton was running across the field. Tracy had never seen him run so fast. She decided she wanted to hear this, so she—with the other players—ran out to the infield. "Don't do this," Coach Carlton was saying to Mr. Klein. "What a terrible example you're setting for the kids."

"Your right fielder trapped the ball," Coach Klein shouted. "I'm not going to put up with—"

"I don't know whether he did or not. I couldn't see it from where I was. But this is the umpire. He has to decide. Now come on, it's still a close game. Your kids have a chance to win it. Don't take that away from them."

"There's no point in playing if the umpires won't call a fair game."

Coach Carlton stepped closer to Mr. Klein, who was a much younger man. He put his hand on his shoulder. "Coach, we're here to teach these kids something. That umpire might have made a mistake, for all I know. But

I don't believe for a minute that he's doing anything but trying his best to call it right."

All the kids had gathered around by now. The umpire had walked a little way off. He seemed to be willing to let Coach Carlton calm things down.

Coach Klein was not sputtering and squeaking so much now. "We should have no outs right now," he said. "And he called three on us."

Martin hadn't said a word until now, but he was standing next to Coach Carlton. "I did catch the ball," he said. "Honest. My glove hit the ground, but the ball never did. Maybe from where you were, it looked like I trapped it, but I didn't."

"Yeah, sure," Badger said. "That's what you have to say now."

But Coach Klein said, "Never mind, Elvin." He took a long breath and then took a few seconds to think things over. "All right," he finally said. "The umpire was closer than we were. We just have to live with his decision." He looked back at Coach Carlton and nodded.

"Let's finish the game," Coach Carlton told all the kids. "We've got a good one going."

The Stingrays didn't look all that pleased with the idea, and Tracy was still thinking the forfeit might have been nice, but everyone cleared the field and the game went on. And once Tracy had time to think about it, she was proud of her coach. The man always stuck to his principles. He wanted to win games, but he cared even more about doing the right thing—and teaching the players to do the same.

When the Scrappers were all back in the dugout, Coach Carlton walked over to them. "Kids, let's leave no doubt who the better team is. What do you say? Should we get some runs?"

Tracy liked that idea. She wasn't in the game, but she wanted to see her team play some ball. It had not been a great game for anyone, but it was time to break out and prove to the Stingrays what a real *team* could do.

Thurlow was up first. He didn't go for the fence this time. He played a good leadoff role and smacked a line drive into left for a single.

Wilson also waited for a good pitch and then drove a hard shot past the shortstop. Thurlow played it safe and stopped at second.

Tracy could feel what was happening.

Everyone wanted to come through for the coach. He had passed up a chance to win the game by forfeit, and he had put his faith in the team. Now, they all wanted to prove he was right.

Bennett was losing some of the pop off his fastball, but even more, he was getting frustrated. After Wilson's hit, he kicked at the pitching rubber and slugged his glove. Now, he looked for his sign. Tracy saw Badger set the target outside, but Bennett ignored that. He fired a fastball right at Trent's head.

Trent twisted away, but the ball smacked him in the shoulder.

At the same instant, the umpire behind the plate shouted, "Pitcher, you're ejected from this game and suspended for the rest of the season."

"So what?" Bennett yelled back at him, and he walked off the mound.

Trent was still on the ground. He was rubbing his shoulder, and the park was silent. Coach Carlton was on his way to check on him. But Trent got up. "I'm okay," he said. And then he trotted to first base.

Tracy watched the Stingrays. A couple of the guys on the bench gave Bennett high fives.

They were laughing and congratulating him as though he had done something great. Coach Klein turned to them and said something, probably telling them to lay off. But it was too late now. He had created a lot of the problems on that team. He should have stopped Bennett's and Badger's big mouths a long time ago.

Tracy was glad she was a Scrapper.

CHAPTER FIVE

The bases were loaded, and Cindy was up to bat. Reynolds was taking over for Bennett on the mound. He was a decent pitcher, even though he didn't pitch very often. He didn't have Bullet's power, but he did throw strikes. Suddenly Tracy wished she were still out there. She really believed she could hit Reynolds, and this would have been her chance to be a hero.

Cindy seemed nervous, but she took her stance, waited, and took a called strike. The ball was over the plate without all that much on it, and Cindy was clearly mad at herself for not swinging. She stepped out of the box, looked down, and thought things over. The girl had never had quite such a load on her back.

But the coach was telling her to take it easy.

"Just poke it somewhere. Let's get a run home."

She stepped back in, and Reynolds threw another one over the plate. Cindy took a beautiful, level swing. The ball shot off her bat and glided into center field. It settled in for a base hit, and two runs scored. The Scrappers had finally broken solidly on top, 4 to 1.

Chad came up next, and he also took a good swing at a Reynolds fastball. But he topped the ball a little and sent it rolling out to second base. He got thrown out, but he moved the runners up, and now two were in scoring position again.

Ollie was up. He was still not a great hitter, but he had worked hard to improve. And he looked all business now. Tracy knew how much he wanted to win this game.

Ollie didn't blast a long bomb, but he connected, and he knocked the ball into left field for a single. Another run scored, and all the singles were adding up. It was 5 to 1.

Martin clearly wanted in on the act. He timed one of Reynolds's pitches and stroked the ball to the right side. If it had been a few inches higher, it would have gone for another base hit, but Harris got up in the air and hauled it in.

It didn't matter. Robbie also flew out to left field, but the damage had been done. Ollie got the Stingrays out easily in the seventh, and it was all over.

Coach told them after the game, "I've never been more proud of you kids. You could have lost your cool out there tonight and fallen apart, but you didn't let those kids get to you. And in the end, it was our *whole team* that won. Every single one of you contributed tonight."

Tracy knew that was true, but she was sure she had offered the least, and she felt bad about that.

"Now it's up to the Mustangs," Gloria said. "We need them to mess up one more time."

"Sure. They might," the coach said. "But listen, if you kids stick around to watch their game, be careful how you behave. Just be quiet and watch. Or cheer for the Pit Bulls, if you want. But don't put down the Mustangs. They're a fine team." He grinned. "Besides, if we have to play them again, we don't want them mad at us. We've had a hard enough time with them as it is."

"But let's all stay," Wilson said. "We can sit together and have some fun."

Tracy had almost forgotten about her friends. She suddenly realized that they were waiting for her. Tracy didn't know what to do. She wanted to be with the team, but Maria had rented a video, and she was expecting Tracy to come over.

"Do you want to go buy a soda before the game starts?" Gloria asked Tracy. "I'm about dying of thirst."

"Well . . . uh . . ."

"You're not going off with Maria and those girls, are you?"

Tracy and Gloria were still sitting on the grass next to each other. Tracy glanced around and saw that her parents and her friends were standing in a little group over behind the dugout. "I kind of promised them," Tracy said.

"Hey, you heard what Wilson said. The team is going to hang together tonight. That's what we've needed all year. The worst thing you could do is run off right now."

Tracy knew Gloria was right. She also felt she had let the team down enough already that evening. She decided that she just had to stay. "Okay," she said, "I'll tell them I'm sticking around."

Gloria gave her a little punch on the shoulder. "Good decision," she said. "You don't need to hang out with those little snobs anyway. I don't know how you can stand them."

"They're okay." The truth was, when Tracy was on the ball field, Maria and the others seemed a little silly to her, too, but they weren't as bad as Gloria thought they were.

Tracy jumped up and ran around the fence to her parents and the girls. As she approached, she said, "I have to stay for a little while. The team agreed to go watch this next game together. If the Mustangs lose, we still have a chance for the championship."

"Do you really *have* to stay?" Maria asked.

"Well, pretty much. It's kind of hard to explain. It's more about team unity—and stuff like that—than about anyone making me stay."

"But what about the video?" Maria asked.

"Can you wait a little while for that? Or, no. Go ahead and start it. That's okay. I'll pick up on what's going on."

Tracy's parents had listened to all this without saying anything. Finally, Mrs. Matlock said, "How are you going to get home?"

"I don't know. All the kids are staying. I can probably catch a ride with someone—or I can just walk."

"No. I don't want you doing that," Mr. Matlock said. "Not alone. Call me if you don't get a ride."

"But, Tracy, I don't see why you have to do this," Mrs. Matlock said.

"I do," Mr. Matlock said. "She's right to stay. I wish the team had started doing things like that a long time ago."

Tracy glanced at Maria, who was looking at Kim and Heather with an "oh, give me a break" look. Maria had no idea what Tracy's father was trying to say. Tracy didn't think she could ever explain it to her, either.

"Well, come over as soon as you can, and we'll wait to start the movie," Maria said. "And by the way, you played great."

"Not really. That was probably the worst game I've played all year."

Maria shrugged, as if she had no idea how to judge.

But Heather said, "Cindy was the big star tonight, wasn't she? Your dad said she made a triple-decker, or something like that."

"What about Martin?" Maria said. "He's the one who caught the ball that one time."

"Well, yeah," Tracy said. "Those two usually don't—" But she stopped herself. She didn't want to put them down. They *had* come through.

"What was everyone so mad about?" Kim asked.

"The Stingrays have some real jerks on their team," Tracy said. "You don't see our pitchers throwing at batters and stuff like that."

"It looked to me like *everyone* was mad. I don't know why you even want to play."

"Kim, you need to come some other time. You need to see how great it is when a team really works together. Did you see, in that last inning, when all our players were stroking the ball, moving runners, driving runs in? That was so—"

Maria giggled, stopping Tracy short. "I think we missed that part. We went down to buy a soda, and we met some boys we know."

"Yeah. Do you know James Wayment? He plays for one of the teams. He was wearing—"

"Look, I have to go," Tracy said. "I'll see you guys in a little while."

She ran back around the fence. When she got there, she found Gloria waiting but looking a little put out. "Come on," she said. "The game is at the north diamond. The other players are already heading over there. What were the little rich girls telling you?"

"Gloria, your dad has a business, the same as theirs. Why do you keep saying that?"

"I don't live in a fancy house in Mountain Oaks."

"So what? I don't care about that."

"Yeah, right."

"Did I go with them, or am I staying with the team?"

Gloria didn't answer. She hurried off toward the other players, and Tracy had to jog to keep up.

As it turned out, the Scrappers had a great time. Justin Lou was pitching for the Mustangs, and he had a terrible night. The Mustangs didn't look like themselves. They gave up four runs in the first inning, and they never really competed. The Pit Bulls were hammering the ball and won going away, 9 to 3.

"The Mustangs won't play like that when we have to face them," Tracy told Gloria, as the game was winding down.

"I know. Salinas will pitch, for one thing," Gloria said. "But, hey, we've got a shot now. If we beat the Hot Rods next week, we can still win the whole thing. Man, that would be so great."

"Even if we don't beat the Mustangs, it's still been a good season. The team has . . ."

"What?"

"Don't get me wrong. I want to win. I'm just saying, we've come so far this season, and—"

"I don't want to hear this. We can't think about anything but winning the *championship*. That's what sports are all about. You can't settle for second—not if you're a winner. You better not go into this next game thinking second is all right."

"Hey, I'll play as hard as I can."

"Or will you worry about getting another black eye?"

Tracy couldn't believe it. "You never let up, do you, Gloria?" she said.

"I don't care. What I care about is that you

keep your eyes on the ball—and don't turn your head again."

"Shut up, all right? Just get off my back."

Tracy got up and walked away, her good mood spoiled. She had had such a great feeling about the team tonight. Gloria—and her big mouth—could always ruin anything. What really bothered Tracy was the fear that Gloria might be right. Maybe Tracy was too afraid of getting hit again to give her all to the game. She certainly didn't care as much about winning as Gloria did. Was that what baseball was all about? If it was, maybe she should make her mother happy and quit the game. The thought depressed her.

Tracy had planned to get a ride home with Gloria's dad, who had promised to stop by for them. But now Tracy didn't want that, so she walked to a pay phone behind the bleachers and called her father. When she got home, she showered and was just about to leave for Maria's when she realized she didn't want to go. She just felt too rotten. What she wanted to do was call Gloria and patch things up. They had been friends for such a long time.

But she couldn't quite bring herself to do that. She was still thinking about quitting baseball, and she knew she couldn't get into that with Gloria.

CHAPTER SIX

On the following morning—a Saturday—Tracy got up late. When she walked out to the kitchen, she found her parents sipping herbal tea and sharing the morning newspaper. "So what are you guys doing today?" Tracy asked.

"I've got to mow the lawn and do some yard work," her dad said. "Want to help me pull some weeds in the flower gardens?"

"It's what I dream about," Tracy said. "I was hoping you'd ask."

"Just for an hour or so. Then you can do whatever you want the rest of the day."

"Actually, I don't have anything to do," Tracy said. She pulled a couple of slices from a loaf of bread on the counter and stuck them in the toaster. It was some multigrain stuff that tasted like it was full of sticks, but Tracy was used to it. Her dad brought it home all the time.

"Tracy," her mom said, "I don't understand why you didn't go over to Maria's last night. Weren't they waiting for you?"

"I called Maria. I told her I was too tired."

"Aren't you feeling well, honey?"

"I'm okay." The toast popped up. Tracy grabbed the slices, set them on a cutting board, and began to spread butter on them.

"Tracy, those girls are all so nice. If you snub them like that, they're not going to invite you again."

Tracy knew what her mother was hoping: that Tracy would become closer friends with Maria and stop spending so much time with Gloria and her sports friends.

"Mom, they didn't even watch the game last night."

"They did at first, but you know how baseball is. Not much happens most of the time. They just lost interest. It was so unpleasant last night anyway, with everyone shouting at each other."

Mr. Matlock had his reading glasses on. He

glanced toward Tracy with his magnified eyes, and he smiled. Then he took the glasses off and said, "Helen, some great things happened in that game."

"Don't start again," her mom said, but she laughed. "I've heard enough jock talk from you and your daughter."

"Well, let me put it this way. Tracy is learning a lot of things that will help her all through life."

"Maybe she could learn the same lessons doing something else—something that doesn't get her all banged up."

"Maybe not. It's not such a bad thing to find out what you're made of."

"Oh, brother." Mom looked at Tracy and rolled her eyes—but she was still smiling. "Your dad still thinks he's in college, playing quarterback, or whatever it was."

"I was a linebacker, my dear. And a hard-nosed one at that." He laughed. "That's where I learned my graceful manner."

Tracy was standing by the counter. She was holding her toast, nibbling at it a little. "I might quit baseball after this year," she said.

Mr. and Mrs. Matlock both looked up from

the table. "Really?" her mom said, and Tracy could hear the heightened interest in her voice.

"Why?" her dad asked.

But Tracy wasn't sure why. She had thought she knew last night, but she couldn't explain it. At the time, she was sick of Gloria and her "must win" attitude. And she was still worried about the next time a ball came flying at her face. But she didn't want to give her mother the pleasure of hearing her criticize Gloria, and she didn't want to admit to her dad that she was afraid of a baseball.

"I don't know," Tracy said. "Maybe I'm just getting tired of putting so much time into it. I kept getting better for a long time, but lately, I feel like I'm not playing very well."

"Honey," her dad said, "that shot you took in the face is bound to set you back for a little while. But you're a fine player, and that team of yours has developed into a thing of beauty. If all you kids stay together next year, it'll be great to see what you can do."

Tracy had thought the same thing. But now she wasn't sure what she would do.

"There's another side to all that," Mrs. Matlock said. "Playing against boys is fine when you're younger, but they're all getting bigger now, and there comes a time when girls just can't compete."

"I can compete," Tracy said.

"That's right," her dad agreed. "Baseball isn't about being big. It's about quickness and good coordination. And as much as anything, it's about using your head." He gave his own head a little knock with his knuckles.

"Knock on wood," his wife replied. But then she said, more carefully, "Tracy, I think it's great that you like to play sports. I just don't want you to become too tough and combative."

"You mean, like Gloria?"

"Well, yes."

Suddenly Tracy felt defensive—even though she had been feeling the same way about Gloria. "There's nothing wrong with being tough—as long as you're not a jerk about it."

"There's nothing wrong with a little gentleness either."

Tracy knew what her mother meant. "Gloria's got some of that in her, too," Tracy said. "You just never see that side of her."

"I guess not," Mrs. Matlock said, and she let the subject go.

A little later, when Tracy and her dad were pulling weeds in front of the house, her dad said, "Honey, I think you're having a wonderful experience playing for a great coach—and learning to play with a team. If you're really not sure you want to play next year, think about it some more once the season is over. But for right now, I'd give these last games your full commitment."

"I will," Tracy told him.

Over the weekend, she thought a lot about what she wanted to do, but at practice on Monday, she concentrated mainly on watching the ball into her glove. She wanted to prove to herself—and Gloria—that she wasn't afraid.

But the coach wasn't hitting those bullets at her that she sometimes got in a game. She still didn't know how she would behave when she had to face one of those.

What she did love was the way the team was working. All the players were psyched up, and they were having fun. Thurlow, who at one time hadn't even wanted to play for the Scrappers, was running hard to chase down every fly ball, taking batting practice seriously, even talking about beating the Hot Rods. "We haven't come this far just to lose now," Tracy heard him tell Wilson. "I want another shot at the Mustangs."

Everyone else seemed to feel the same way. The Hot Rods were tough. Oates and Rohrbach were both good pitchers, and they had a lot of team speed. The Scrappers had lost to them before. Tracy worried that the Scrappers might get too uptight just because they couldn't stand the thought of losing.

When Coach Carlton called the players together at the end of practice, he looked happy. "You're playing really well right now, kids," he said. "This has been a thrill for me. Win or lose tomorrow night, I've enjoyed working with you."

When Coach told the kids they could go, Gloria stood up. Tracy was still sitting on the grass. "I wish the coach wouldn't say things like that," Gloria said.

"Like what?" Tracy asked. She glanced up at Gloria.

"'Win or lose.' We can't even think about losing. We just have to pay the price, do whatever it takes. There's no way we can lose that game."

"If you keep talking that way, you'll just be all nervous when the game starts. I think we're better off going out there and playing, not telling ourselves how *terrible* it will be if we lose."

"Are you crazy, Tracy? This is it. This is what we've been playing for all summer. I want the trophy. I want to show the Mustangs they're not better than us."

"I want to win, too. But it's not the end of the world if we don't."

"*What?* Don't you *care* if we lose?"

Tracy ducked her head. Gloria was yelling now, and the kids who were still around were all looking over to see what was going on. "That's not what I said," Tracy told Gloria.

"Well, don't tell me it doesn't matter if we lose."

"She said it's not the end of the world. And it isn't."

But this was not from Tracy. It was from the coach. He walked over to Gloria. "We might try our best and still lose. There's no shame in that. Baseball is a funny game. There's a lot of luck in it. And the Hot Rods are good. We just need to play hard, enjoy the game, and see how it turns out."

"I don't buy that," Gloria said. "I *promise* you, we're going to win. I don't know about everyone else, but I'm going to do whatever it takes. No one is going to get me out. And Tracy better not bail out on any more ground balls."

"Gloria," Coach said, "you've come a long way this season. Don't slip back. Don't start criticizing."

"I'm not criticizing her. I'm trying to kick her butt—and get her going. But she's acting like her friends over on the *nice* side of town." Gloria grabbed her athletic bag and walked to her bike. Then she got on and pumped away.

The coach crouched down in front of Tracy. "What was that all about?" he asked.

"It's just Gloria. You know how she is."

"Are you feeling afraid since you got hit?" he asked her.

"Sometimes. Yeah."

"Remember, the worst thing you can do is look away. That makes the ball *more* dangerous, not less."

"I know. But I do it without meaning to."

"Do you want me to hit some more to you?"

"Hard ones?"

"Yes."

"I don't know. I . . ."

"If you don't get over it, you'll never play really well again."

"I might quit. I'm not sure I want to play anymore."

"Don't leave the game because you're scared. Leave it when the time is right. Let me hit a few to you right now."

Tracy took a deep breath. She thought it over for maybe half a minute, and then she said, "Okay. Let's do it."

CHAPTER SEVEN

Coach Carlton started slow. He hit some easy grounders to Tracy. He reminded her each time to look the ball into her glove. Gradually, he increased his bat speed until he was hammering some tough shots at her. She didn't field every one of them cleanly, but she never looked away, and she felt good about that. Coach kept telling her, "That's it. That's the way. All you need is to get your confidence back."

But just when Tracy thought she was over her fears, Coach hit a ball that took a bad hop. The ball came up suddenly and higher than Tracy expected. She reacted well with her hands and actually gloved the ball. But as soon as she had made the stop, she realized what had happened. She had turned her head.

She looked at the coach, then down at the grass. "I did it again," she said.

"I know. But that's all right. You've been fine on all the others. Let's hit some more." So the coach knocked some more at her, and she handled them well. He praised her the whole time, but she knew that she had lost her nerve on the scariest ball he had hit. What would she do if something like that happened in the game?

When the coach finally let her go, Tracy got on her bike, but she didn't feel like going straight home. She took a little extra ride around her neighborhood. She wanted to talk to someone, but she wasn't sure who would understand. Maria certainly wouldn't, and Gloria was the last person she wanted to talk to right now. She found herself riding by Martin's house. She would never have gone in, but she saw him outside. He was sitting on his front porch reading a book.

She stopped her bike and said, "Hey, Martin."

He hadn't noticed her until then. But he immediately set his book down and walked out to the curb. "Hi," he said. "Did the coach work with you for a while?"

"Yeah."

"Did it go okay?"

"Well . . . yeah. Mostly."

"Your black eye is clearing up pretty fast now."

She laughed. "Yeah. It'll be okay in a few more days—if I don't get hit again."

"Are you worried about that?"

Tracy knew she had led him into asking that question. It was what she wanted to talk about. But she was also not sure she dared. "I guess I am. Some. It doesn't seem like I am, but then I kind of flinch every now and then."

"Man, I used to do that *every* time. It always seemed like the ball was going to hit me right between the eyes. That's one reason I'd rather play in the outfield."

"It usually doesn't bother me. Just now— since I got hit." Tracy was still standing with her leg over her bike.

"Hey, if someone throws a ball at your head, you duck. It's just a natural reaction."

"If you have the confidence, you don't duck. You grab the ball before it hits you."

"Yeah, I guess. But you're a better fielder

than I'll ever be. A better player." He stuck his hands in the back pockets of his shorts, and he smiled. He didn't seem to mind admitting to that.

"You've improved a lot this year."

"Sure. But I'll never be as good as you."

"Do you mean that?"

"Sure, I do."

"Doesn't that bother you?"

"No. Why should it?"

"I don't know. Gloria wouldn't be able to handle it if she thought I was better than her." Tracy finally swung her leg down from her bike.

Martin seemed to be thinking. "I don't know," he finally said. "Gloria knows Thurlow is better than she is, and that doesn't seem to bother her. It just drives her nuts when people don't play as well as they can."

"But who can do that? How can we be at our very best all the time?"

"Maybe we can't. Gloria just wants us to *try*—and never let up, not for a second."

"I know. But what can I do, Martin? I don't mean to turn my head. It just happens."

"The more you think about it, the worse it

will be. Just let go. Play like you always have before."

Tracy nodded. "Yeah. That's right. I've been thinking way too much. But, Martin, no matter how hard we try, we could lose this next game— or we could lose to the Mustangs. If I'm the one who messes things up, Gloria will hate me."

"Maybe. I don't know. But if she does, that's her problem, not yours."

Tracy nodded. She had to agree. But she still didn't want to let the team down.

At the park the next day, Gloria came over to Tracy immediately. Tracy expected the worst. But Gloria said, "Listen, Trace, I've been thinking about what we talked about. You were right, in a way. So was the coach. If I get all uptight— and start screaming at everybody—I'm going to blow everything. So I'm going to cool it and just play hard. But sometimes winning *is* about refusing to lose—finding a way to get the job done. Let's get it done tonight, okay?"

"Okay. But . . ."

"But what?"

"I'm not sure I won't have trouble again."

"Tracy, I've watched you go from good to great this year. You can do anything I can do. And I never thought you would be that good."

"Really? You think I'm as good as you are?"

"I have more power than you do, but you have better bat control. I have a stronger arm, but you get to the ball quicker. So we're pretty much even. And you know me. I wouldn't say that if I didn't mean it."

"Wow. That's great. I didn't think you felt that way."

"Hey, I can be nice. I just don't want to get too much in the habit of it."

"So are you just—?"

"No. I mean it. Every word. You can be every bit as good as I am, if you just play the way I do. When the ball comes to me, I think I'm going to do something spectacular with it. Every now and then I boot one, but I don't say to myself, 'Maybe I'm not any good.' I say, 'That was weird. I won't do that again.' And that's exactly what I believe."

"I'll never be that confident."

"Don't say that. Just expect to do great things tonight."

"All right. I'll try."

"The Mustangs won this afternoon, so we have to win to stay alive."

"Okay. But, Gloria, remember what the coach said. Things happen in a baseball game. We could play our very best and still lose."

"I know. I can live with that." Then she grinned. "I just don't want to."

That was something Tracy could agree with.

The game was under the lights, and a big crowd was already arriving—not just parents but a lot of other players from the league. Everyone knew this would be the last game of the season if the Scrappers lost. The Mustangs were there in force. Billy Mauer, the Mustangs' second baseman, even walked by Tracy while she was stretching and said, "I hope you guys win."

"You do?" Tracy said.

"Sure. I want to play another game. And I want to whip you guys one more time."

A lot of the Scrappers heard the remark, but no one reacted. They were all pretty quiet tonight. Tracy figured they were trying to stay focused, trying to think about nothing but winning this big game.

The Scrappers were batting first, so after they warmed up they headed for the dugout. When the ump finally called for the game to start, Jeremy took a big breath, smiled at his teammates, and then marched to the plate. The Scrappers were all up and yelling. "Let's get it going *right now!*" Gloria was shouting.

Jake Oates was pitching tonight. He could really *bring* the ball, and he had nothing to lose. The Hot Rods just wanted to prove they were better than the Scrappers, even if they had no chance to win the championship. Oates had been making comments to his friends, and the word had gotten back to the Scrappers that he was *not* going to lose this game.

He sounded like Gloria.

Oates glared at his catcher, got the signal, and then reared way back and came in with a cannonball of a pitch. It looked a little high for Jeremy—at least to Tracy—but the umpire called it a strike.

Tracy could hardly believe the reaction, so many people shouting, disagreeing or agreeing, but everyone was into it. This was going to be a tense night.

The next pitch looked about the same, but it probably was a little lower. Jeremy started a swing, late, and then held up. He looked overpowered, but now he had two strikes on him, and there was no "make him pitch to you" talk from the coach.

But Oates showed off a little. He had Jeremy on his heels, and he should have stayed with his fastball. But he tried to throw a curve, and he hung it high over the plate. Jeremy could have taken ball one, but instead, he reached up and slapped the ball.

Jeremy caught the ball flush, and it darted past Kiesel in left field before he could move over to cut it off. Kiesel did chase it down before it rolled to the fence, but by then Jeremy was zipping toward second. He went in standing up, and the crowd went crazy. Tracy could hear Mr. Corrigan making foghorn noises, and Gloria's dad and brothers were just as loud. They were into this game already.

"Everyone hits. Everyone hits," the Scrappers were all yelling.

Robbie couldn't stand to walk to the plate. He ran. And he set up, ready and eager. The first pitch was outside, and Robbie held up. Ball one.

The next pitch was down in the strike zone. Robbie went after it and missed, but Oates had let Jeremy get a huge lead, and on the pitch, he blasted over to third. He slid in, but Rohrbach, who was catching tonight, didn't even bother to throw to third.

A runner on third with no one out. The Scrappers were looking aggressive out there!

But Oates threw a fireball next, and Robbie popped it up. The ball floated very high, and the first baseman staggered a little as he waited for it. But he didn't let the lights bother him, and he reached up and made the catch. Jeremy had to hold at third.

That brought up Gloria, and she had vowed that no one was going to get her out. She had managed to get dirt all over her pants already, and now she rubbed some on her hands. She cocked her bat and waited, and when Oates threw a good fastball to her, she took that perfect, natural swing of hers and met the thing with all her force.

The ball flashed off her bat like it was hit into the next county. But Eric Fellows, the shortstop, was in the way. He stuck up his glove in self-defense, and the ball smacked into it. The sound of the leather echoed through the park, and Eric actually fell backward, on his seat. But he had the ball.

Two outs.

Gloria blew her breath out in disgust. But she must have thought about the things the coach had told her. She couldn't have tried any harder, couldn't have hit the ball with any more force, but it was just an out.

What the Scrappers had to do was keep hitting shots like that. If they kept connecting, they would score runs. But Thurlow got suckered on a first-pitch curve, and he bounced a ground ball to the first baseman. The Scrappers were out, and they had left the runner at third.

Tracy hated to think that it might be another one of those nights when runs were hard to come by.

CHAPTER EIGHT

Eric Fellows was up first for the Hot Rods. He always made Tracy a little nervous because he was so fast, but she tried to put positive thoughts in her head. She told herself to think about the things Gloria had told her.

All the same, the worry was still lurking in her head. What about a hard shot, hit straight at her? If she looked away tonight, she could disappoint the whole team.

Adam was pitching tonight. Before the game he would hardly speak to anyone. Tracy knew he was really focused and trying to stay that way. But she sensed that he was nervous, too. She knew that, like everyone else, he was saying to himself, "We've *got* to win."

The Hot Rods, on the other hand, were having a great time. They were talking it up in the dugout, laughing, yelling at Fellows to knock Adam off the mound—all the usual stuff. But they had nothing to lose.

Fellows, as it turned out, didn't make good contact. He swung off balance and hit the ball off the end of his bat. But the ball looped toward right field. Tracy raced after it and couldn't reach it. It dropped just over her glove and rolled toward the right field line.

Jeremy ran hard to get to the ball, and he spotted Fellows making a big turn at first. It was something he often did. If he could catch an outfielder sleeping, he would take off for second. But Jeremy shot the ball to Ollie, at first, and Fellows was caught in no-man's-land. He saw immediately that he had no chance to get back to first, so he took off for second. Ollie threw to Gloria, covering the base for Tracy, and Fellows held up. He was trapped in a rundown.

Tracy hustled over to back up Ollie. Gloria ran at Fellows, made him turn back toward first, then threw to Ollie. And Ollie put the tag on Fellows.

Textbook play.

One away. And the coach was yelling, "Smart

play, Jeremy. Way to be thinking out there. Good rundown, kids. Great work."

Tracy was yelling the same thing to Jeremy and Gloria and Adam. She was also remembering what a mess the team had made of plays like that, early in the season.

Brian Kiesel came up next, and he hit a fly ball to left field. Trent got a good jump on the ball, which was hooking toward the left field line. He didn't have much speed, but he had judged the ball just right. He chased it down, reached up, and snagged it with one hand. Two away.

Then big Matt Rohrbach took the plate. He jumped on Adam's first pitch and bounced a grounder to Tracy. It took a nice hop as she charged it. She caught it and made the short toss to first. Nothing to it.

The side was retired, and Tracy felt herself—and the team—relax a little. Jeremy had used his head to keep the Hot Rods from getting something started, and Trent had made a fine catch in left. Maybe Tracy's play was no big deal, but at least she had handled the ball with some confidence.

Robbie gave her a slap on the back as she walked into the dugout. "Nice job," he said.

Tracy almost told him that anyone could handle a ground ball like that one, but she knew what he was really saying. The whole team knew she was struggling, and he was just letting her know he was on her side. "Thanks," she said, and then she sat down next to Gloria.

"Good work," Gloria said. "I saw you cover Ollie. Everyone played that rundown exactly right."

Wilson grabbed a bat and headed to the plate. Oates toyed with him a little, tried to get him to swing at a fastball outside, and then he threw a change-up that stayed too high. But on a 2 and 0 count, he threw the ball down the middle. Wilson swung hard and slugged a low line drive. The ball shot past the center fielder and bounced to the fence.

Big Wilson ran like a train. It took a while to get him going, but once he got to full speed, he could roll right along. He chugged around first, made it to second, and was seriously considering a triple until he saw the coach hold his arms up. So he rounded second and brought himself to a halt. Then he walked back to the bag as the ball finally came flying in from the outfield.

He clapped his hands and waved to the dugout. "All right. This is our inning!" he shouted. "Keep it going."

Trent was up, and Tracy was on deck. As she looked for her bat, she heard voices in the bleachers: "Get a hit, Tracy." She was surprised to see that Maria and Kim and Heather were at the game. She hadn't expected them, didn't think they would ever come again.

Tracy swung her bat a couple of times and then kneeled down. She watched Trent as he took a called strike. Then, on the next pitch, he got fooled on a curve, but he managed to reach out and punch the ball toward the right side of the infield. Kevin Bank, the second baseman, had no chance to get Wilson, who barreled over to third, so he turned and threw out Trent.

Now it was Tracy's job to get Wilson home. Another ground ball might manufacture a run, and that would be good, but what she really wanted was to ignite a big inning. She wanted a base hit.

She took a look at the outfielders. They were moving in on her, but there was a big gap in right center, just waiting, if she could hit the ball there.

Oates's first pitch was like a bolt of lightning. It clapped into Rohrbach's mitt and sent shivers running through Tracy's body.

The pitch had been a little high, and the ump called it a ball, but Tracy was not sure that she could have hit it. She stepped out of the box and shut her eyes. She knew she had gotten hits off this guy before. She could time that fastball. But she was still nervous about him coming inside on her. Could she handle that?

She heard her friends cheering for her, up in the stands, and then she heard Gloria yell, "Poke one, Trace. This guy's no problem."

Tracy stepped back to the plate. She judged the next pitch well. She drove her bat through the ball, nice and smooth. She didn't crush the ball, but she knocked it through that gap. The center fielder cut it off—which held her to a single—but Wilson scored. The Scrappers were on top, 1 to 0.

Tracy's teammates were all cheering for her,

and up in the bleachers, Tracy spotted her mom and dad. Her mother was standing up and clapping, and her father was yelling, "Way to go, Tracy. You're the woman."

A lot of people in the crowd laughed at that, and Tracy was a little embarrassed, but she did feel good. And even more, she was relaxing into the game now, feeling part of it.

She took a good lead and stayed ready. When Adam hit a ground ball to the shortstop, she broke hard for second. She had no chance to beat the throw, but she slid hard and knocked Bank off balance. He had no chance to relay the ball to first for the double play.

So the Scrappers were still alive. As Tracy ran off the field, the coach complimented her on her strong slide. But Ollie went down swinging, and the top of the inning was over.

The Scrappers ran back to the field and, once again, played some great defense. Thurlow ran a long way to catch a fly ball that Josh Meyers hit, and Wilson had to go right to the backstop to field a pop-up off Oates's bat. Then David Dietz worked Adam for a walk, and Ricky Tobias hit a grounder up the middle. It looked like a sure base hit, but Gloria got a great break on it and snagged it with one hand. Tracy had broken toward the ball. She kept going to the bag, and Gloria leaped in the air, turned, and flipped the ball back to her for the force-out.

It was another good inning on defense, but Adam wasn't exactly blowing anyone away. Tracy knew the top of the order was back up now, and she hoped the Scrappers could break loose with some more runs.

As it turned out, the Scrappers didn't exactly "break loose." Jeremy struck out on a 3 and 2 fastball, and Robbie grounded out to the shortstop. But with two outs, Gloria fouled off about four pitches and finally walked. Then Thurlow hit a long shot that looked like a sure home run. It hit short, however, and bounced over the fence for a double. Gloria, by rule, had to stop at third. Wilson followed with a ground ball at the shortstop. It should have been an easy play, but Fellows booted the ball, and Wilson was safe on the error. Gloria scored.

After that, Oates struck out Trent, and the rally was over. Still, the Scrappers were up 2 to 0 going to the bottom of the third. They just had to keep up the good defense and continue finding ways to scrape out runs against Oates.

Bank was up first for the Hot Rods. He wasn't much of a hitter, but Adam made a mistake. He got behind 2 and 0 and then took a little too much off the ball. Bank finally saw a pitch he could hit, and he unloaded on it. He hit a line drive that got past Robbie for a single.

"All right. Still no outs," Gloria yelled. "Take the easy one. Get two if you can."

The batter was a kid named Drew Depola. He usually didn't start for the Hot Rods, and Tracy wasn't sure why he was in the lineup tonight. "Easy out," she shouted. "Just throw the ball by him, Adam."

And that's what Adam did. His first pitch was a little inside. Depola stayed *very* loose after that. He struck out on the next three pitches.

But now the top of the Hot Rod lineup was coming up. Fellows and Kiesel and Rohrbach— three tough outs.

And Fellows got lucky. He swung hard at a fastball, down in the zone. He chopped the ball, and it took a high bounce toward third. Robbie came in for it, but he had to wait for the ball to come down. When it finally did, he gunned the ball to second. But the throw was late.

Tracy wondered whether Robbie shouldn't have thrown to first, but she was sure Robbie had been aware of Fellows's speed. There was probably nothing he could have done. It was just a fluke play.

But now runners were at first and second, and Adam was in a jam for the first time. Still, he kept his concentration. He threw a curve that broke big. Kiesel took a lunge at it and knocked a ground ball toward first. Ollie fielded the ball and looked to second, but Wanda Coates, the first base coach, yelled, "Take one," and Ollie ran to first and took the easy out.

Two away, and Rohrbach up with the tying runs in scoring position. Adam threw a great fastball at the guy's knees. Rohrbach ripped at it and got nothing.

Then Adam wasted a curve outside, probably hoping to get Rohrbach to swing at a bad pitch. But Rohrbach laid off it, and the count was 1 and 1.

Adam's next pitch was hot, but it was out over the plate. Tracy heard the sound of the solid smash, and she didn't even have to look. She knew it was gone.

The ball cleared the left field fence, and after all the great defense, the Scrappers were down, 3 to 2.

The Hot Rods made it seem like the end of the game—the end of the World Series—the way they carried on. It was irritating. But Gloria walked over to Tracy and said, "That's all right. We're okay. We can hit Oates. We're going to win this game."

Tracy felt the confidence, believed it. And then she watched as Gloria walked toward Adam. Tracy knew she was telling Adam the same thing. He nodded, and then he threw a great pitch to Meyers, got him out on a weak grounder back to the pitcher's mound.

As Tracy ran off the field, she could feel some butterflies in her stomach, but she also remembered the confidence. Gloria was turning into a real leader, and maybe her sheer will could get the Scrappers back on top.

CHAPTER NINE

Tracy led off the fourth inning and met the ball perfectly, but she drove it right at the center fielder. He stood his ground and made the catch. Then Adam struck out. But Ollie stayed with an Oates curveball and knocked it into left field. Jeremy followed with a walk.

With two outs and two on, Robbie had a chance to pull the Scrappers even or put them back in the lead. He hit the ball hard, too, but he spanked a ground ball to the left, and Fellows made a great play on it. He ran hard to his right, and with his momentum going the wrong way, had to make a quick throw across his body to catch Robbie at first, who had good speed. The ball popped into Meyers's glove, just in time, and the Scrappers were out.

"We've got ourselves a great game going," Coach Carlton yelled. "This is fun. Let's shut them down this time."

Tracy wanted to win, but she understood what the coach was saying. It was great to see two teams play well and really compete for the victory. She had to respect the Hot Rods for the way they were battling even though they had so much less at stake.

Adam faced Oates, Dietz, and Tobias in the bottom of the fourth. He seemed to be getting stronger as the game went on, and he was putting the ball right into Wilson's glove, no matter where Wilson set the target. He struck out Oates and Dietz, and Tobias only ticked the ball and dropped it in front of the plate. Wilson grabbed it and tossed Tobias out before he was halfway to first base.

As the Scrappers ran off the field this time, Gloria yelled at her teammates, "All right. Now we do it. We break this thing open." She got a bat immediately and stood outside the batter's box as Oates warmed up. She timed her practice swings to his speed, and Tracy could see how much that irritated Oates.

"Don't try to look so *bad*," Oates yelled to

her. "You know you can't hit me."

"Just pitch the ball," Gloria said. The words came out almost as a growl, and everyone in the park must have heard her. Tracy could never bait a pitcher like that, but Gloria stepped into the box, obviously ready to back up what she said.

The first pitch was high, and Gloria took a reckless swing at it. She missed it completely, and all the Hot Rods got on her. "Oooh, you're so tough, Gloria," Dietz yelled at her.

But Gloria was paying no attention. She stepped away from the plate, ducked her head, gripped the bat, took a long breath, and then stepped back and dug in. The next pitch was probably low, but Gloria took a better swing this time—a smooth stroke—and she *banged* the ball, solid. The ring of aluminum sounded through the air.

Tracy jumped up to see where the ball was heading. It took off on a hard line drive, and then it started to rise. It was only just leveling off as it passed over the fence for a home run.

The Scrappers were stunned for a moment as they watched the ball sail out of the park. Gloria had never hit a ball that hard, that long. "What a *shot!"* Thurlow whispered. And then everyone ran out to home plate.

Gloria forgot to trot. She darted around the bases, and she raised her hands in the air as she headed home. Everyone was ready with high fives. Gloria loved all that, but she was yelling, "That's just the start. Let's keep it going now."

Tracy knew that was right. The score was tied, 3 to 3, but the Scrappers needed to get a good lead. She might get up this inning, and she had to contribute something, the way Gloria had done.

Thurlow was up after Gloria. Tracy felt that he had been putting too much pressure on himself to hit home runs. But this time up, he didn't overswing. He kept his balance, timed his pitch, and met Oates's fastball. He hit the ball hard enough to knock it downtown, but it was a low line shot. It whizzed by Fellows's head so fast that the guy had no time to react. It reached Kiesel in left field on one bounce, and Thurlow had to hold up with a single.

But it was good to see Thurlow driving the ball again. Tracy felt pretty sure that he was coming out of his slump.

Wilson was up next, and he also took a nice swing at the ball. He hit another hard blow at Fellows, but on the ground. It was a perfect double-play ball, and Tracy held her breath. But Thurlow got a great jump, and he flashed toward second. Fellows saw that and didn't even try to get him. He went straight to first and gunned down Wilson.

Trent was up, and Tracy was on deck. She walked out, got her bat, and then took a knee. She watched Oates. She had been noticing the pattern of his throws all night. He loved to come inside with a pitch and then follow with a curveball. But his curve often hung in the air, and she was pretty sure that was the pitch she had the best chance to hit.

Oates threw a fastball to Trent, and he laced it hard down the left field line. But Tobias, at third base, stuck up his glove, and the ball banged into it. Tracy couldn't believe what was happening. Everyone was timing Oates now, but runs were still hard to get.

Now it was Tracy's chance to do something about that. As she walked to the plate, she heard her parents, her neighborhood friends, her teammates, and above all, Gloria—all screaming at her to get a hit. But she could also hear the Hot Rods riding her, and even the Mustangs who were in the crowd. "You better duck, Tracy," one of them yelled, "or Oates will black your other eye."

Tracy stepped into the box, and then almost immediately, she threw up her hand and said, "Wait a sec, ump," and she backed out. She was hearing all the voices, not concentrating. She shut her eyes, tried to forget about everything but Oates and what she wanted to do.

With Thurlow at second, and with his speed, a single was almost sure to produce the go-ahead run. Oates almost always started with a fastball, and Rohrbach usually set up outside. She decided she would take the first pitch unless Oates happened to groove one for her. She stepped back in, and this time, she tried to think of nothing but that ball in Oates's hand.

Oates nodded to the sign, and he looked all business. He wasn't bragging now, just bearing down. He threw a fastball, outside, just as Tracy had guessed, and she let it go. Ball one.

But now he liked to come inside. And that gave Tracy a funny feeling. Oates could really hum the ball, and she didn't want to have to face one of those.

Oates was pitching from the stretch with a man on, but he reached way back and brought the ball *hard*. Tracy was backing away almost before he let go of the pitch.

But the ball was right down the middle. She was out of position, and she had to let it go by. Strike one.

"Come on, Tracy. Stand in there," Gloria yelled.

Tracy was ashamed. Maybe most people didn't know what she had done, but Gloria had seen it, and surely the coach had. Oates had certainly seen her stepping away, too. He would probably come with his curve now.

She dug in, and she told herself to wait on the curve—not to bail out if the pitch looked like it was coming at her.

Oates gave the ball a big motion again and fired it right at her. Tracy held her ground, and then—suddenly—she knew it was a fastball. She twisted away just as the ball rocketed past her head.

Tracy stepped away and took a long breath.

She didn't think Oates had thrown at her. He was only busting her inside so he could throw his curve this time. The next pitch was the one she was waiting for.

But she was still breathing hard. The ball hadn't missed her head by more than an inch or two.

Tracy felt the quiet in the Scrappers' dugout, as though her teammates were frightened for her. But she told herself this was the moment of truth. She had to hold her ground and not let this next one scare her into bailing out again.

Sure enough, the next pitch was inside, but Tracy waited, saw the spin of the ball. As the curve bent, it hung out over the plate—just as she had hoped it would. She took a good, quick swing and jabbed the ball up the middle. It landed in center field, and Tracy had a base hit.

Thurlow charged home like a racehorse heading for the finish line. The Scrappers were on top, and Tracy had done more than drive a run in. She had frightened away a few demons in her head. She felt as though she could face anything now.

She stood at first and looked across the diamond. Her teammates were cheering, and her friends in the bleachers were clapping and shouting. She hadn't felt this good in a long time.

But Adam hit the ball in the air to right field, and Dietz made the catch. The Scrappers had a one-run lead again, 4 to 3, but the Hot Rods weren't going away.

As Tracy trotted across the diamond, Gloria ran toward her. She was bringing Tracy her glove. As she handed it to Tracy, she grinned. "Great job," she said. "You didn't let that big guy scare you. You stayed right in there."

"I think I'm over my fears now," Tracy told her.

"That's obvious. You're tough, Trace—the toughest rich girl I know."

"Gloria, lay off that. I'm tired of hearing it."

"Hey, I'm just kidding."

"No, you're not."

Gloria looked at the ground. "Look, Trace, I don't like those girls who've been coming to our games lately. They think they're better than me."

"I don't think they do, Gloria. But it doesn't

matter what they think. You and I have been friends forever, and we always will be."

Gloria nodded. "All right," she said. "I'll lay off the 'rich girl' stuff."

"Okay." The girls slapped their gloves together and then ran to their positions.

Tracy felt a lot better, but she knew this might be her last inning before Cindy replaced her in the lineup. She wanted to come through on defense the way she had on offense.

Angela Hobart was in the game now for Kevin Bank. But she was clearly overpowered by Adam's fastball. She watched a couple of strikes go by, and then she took a late swing and missed.

Great start. But Adam missed with a couple of fastballs to Depola, and after he fouled off some pitches, Adam walked him. That was only Adam's second walk today. Tracy wasn't worried about that. Adam was staying focused.

What Tracy did think about was the speed she was now dealing with. Depola could run very well, and Fellows was up. A double play would be tough, and any little mistake could lead to big trouble.

Fellows foul tipped the first pitch. But then he slapped a stinging ground ball straight at Tracy. It hit close and came up hard.

Tracy reacted quickly, but the ball got over her glove and slammed against her shoulder. It dropped in front of her, and she grabbed it. She knew that it was too late to think about a double play, so she tossed the ball hard to first—in time to get Fellows.

As soon as the ball popped into Ollie's glove, Tracy felt the pain. She had taken a hard slug in the shoulder, and she knew she was going to have a huge bruise, but she didn't want anyone to know she was hurting. She walked back to her position, tried to show no emotion in her face. She wanted to stay in the game as long as she could.

Gloria was running toward her. "Are you all right?" she asked.

"Sure." Tracy turned away and looked toward the outfield.

"Where did it hit you?"

"In the shoulder. It's all right."

Gloria stepped around her, so the girls were looking at each other. "Tracy, that ball just came up on you. You didn't turn your head. You stayed right with it."

"I know."

"It was a great play."

"We might have gotten two if I hadn't booted the ball."

"Hey, they could have had two runners on if you hadn't taken a bullet for the team. You could have ducked away, but you didn't."

Tracy nodded. She knew that was true.

"Tracy, I was kidding before. You're as tough as *anyone* out here."

Tracy laughed. That *wasn't* true. Not really. But she thought maybe she was tough enough, and she liked the idea.

The coach was on his way out, but as Gloria ran back to her position, she yelled to him that Tracy was all right. He hesitated, but then Tracy said, "Really. I'm fine." Coach nodded and walked back to his box.

The Hot Rods still had a man on—in scoring position. But when Kiesel hit a line drive toward left, Gloria jumped high and pulled it down.

The fifth inning was over, and the Scrappers still had their one-run lead.

CHAPTER TEN

The Scrappers were yelling that they were going to get Oates this time. And then above the other voices, Jeremy shouted, "He's not pitching. Rohrbach is."

Everyone turned to see big Rohrbach hum a warm-up pitch at Oates, who was now catching. Rohrbach had gotten tougher all year, and he was another big guy who could throw some real artillery.

Tracy heard the voices around her soften. Everyone was saying, "Ah, we can hit him," but they all knew Rohrbach's arm would be fresh, and they had just started to time Oates's hard stuff.

Ollie was up first, and he didn't do much to

build confidence. He swung late on a Rohrbach fastball. He rolled the ball to Meyers at first base, who picked the ball up and stepped on the bag for the out.

Then Jeremy tried to poke the ball but only nubbed it as far as Hobart, at second base. She caught it for out number two. Robbie did no better. He sent a ground ball hopping toward the shortstop. Fellows gloved it and threw him out.

Rohrbach had only thrown five pitches, and the Scrappers were already heading back to the field. Tracy thought for sure she would be pulled at that point, but Coach put Cindy in for Ollie. He sent Chad to left, for Trent, and Martin to right field, for Jeremy.

As Martin ran toward right field, he passed Tracy. "Let's get 'em, Martin," she told him.

"I hope I don't mess up," he said.

"Hey, don't say that. You've looked great out there lately."

Gloria walked over to Tracy and said, "The coach left you in for a reason. You're coming through today. He's got confidence in you. Just keep concentrating."

"I will." And Tracy knew what she meant. She couldn't let her fears bother her—even with the pain in her shoulder. She could feel that shoulder tightening up, but her throwing arm was okay, and she told herself not to worry.

When Tracy took up her position, it certainly wasn't hard to keep her head in the game. Rohrbach was up. All Tracy could think of was that home run he had hit the last time.

Tracy watched Wilson's signal. She was surprised to see him call for a change-up. It seemed a huge gamble, but Adam nodded, and then he used his fastball motion as he released a palm-ball change-up.

The ball floated toward the plate, and Rohrbach started a big swing, then tried to slow it down. The ball clicked off the end of his bat and rolled straight back to Adam.

Adam threw the big guy out, and Tracy hoped that was the last time the Scrappers would have to see Rohrbach at bat. Meyers followed, and then big Oates, but Adam got them both on ground balls.

So the game went to the seventh, and the

whole season was riding on one inning. "We've *got* to get some more runs," Thurlow told everyone. Tracy could feel that he was completely a part of the team now.

Gloria was up first. She took a strike but then worked the count to 3 and 1 before she slammed a ball straight back at Rohrbach. It was a dagger, and it was headed right at his nose, but he got his glove up and fought it off. The ball glanced off his mitt, and for a moment Tracy thought Gloria would be on base. But the ball bounced straight to Hobart, at second, and she threw Gloria out.

"I can't believe how lucky these guys are," Robbie said. "We can't get a break."

Tracy was thinking the same thing. The Scrappers had hit the ball hard all day, and they had very little to show for it. Gloria had vowed not to let anyone get her out—but there was only so much she could do about that.

Thurlow clearly wanted to change the run of luck. He watched as Rohrbach threw an outside fastball, and then, with his quick wrists, he *whipped* the next pitch into center field. The center fielder had to chase the ball, and even though he cut it off, Thurlow turned on his speed and dashed to second.

Then Wilson hit a ball hard, but it lifted high in the air for a long out. At least Thurlow tagged up and darted over to third.

Chad was up, and Tracy walked out to the on-deck area. She wasn't about to tell anyone, but as she swung her bat, she felt a lot of pain. She knew she was only bruised. Swinging a bat couldn't hurt her, but she wondered whether the pain and stiffness would slow her swing. Maybe she should tell the coach.

But Chad swung at the first pitch and popped the ball up. The third baseman ran into foul territory and made the catch.

So Tracy wouldn't bat, and the Scrappers had left Thurlow on third. Now the game came down to three outs. Tracy ran back to the field. She kept rolling her shoulder, trying to keep it loose.

She saw Gloria trotting toward her. "You're hurting, aren't you?" she said.

"A little. I'll be okay."

"Don't stay in the game if you can't play. The rule says that the coach can put a player back in the lineup in the case of an injury. Ollie could go back to first, and Cindy could switch to second."

"It's my left shoulder. It's sore and kind of stiff, but my throwing arm is fine."

"But what if you have to handle a hard grounder? Won't you worry about getting that shoulder hit again?"

"No. I'll be okay."

"Then stay in the game, Trace. We need you out here."

"Thanks, Glor."

Gloria returned to her position, and Tracy got ready for Adam to throw his first pitch to Dietz. The tension in the park was unbelievable. Just as things quieted a little, and Adam took his sign, Tracy heard someone yell, "Keep it up, Tracy. You're doing great."

Tracy realized that it was Maria. The three girls were still up there in the bleachers, but Tracy had forgotten all about them. She could see that they were watching, not wandering off like in the Stingrays game.

Adam wasn't giving an inch. His first pitch was the hardest fastball he had thrown all night. It was out over the plate, but Dietz let it go by. When he got another one, just like the last, he tried to go after it, but he foul tipped it. And then he whiffed on a pitch that was actually off the plate, outside.

One down.

Tracy took a long breath. Maybe Adam could strike out the side, and she wouldn't have to make a play.

But Tobias got lucky. He stuck his bat out, and the ball hit it. It looped to the right side, over Tracy. Martin ran hard and held the hit to a single, but now the tying run was on.

Hobart came up next. She swung and missed, then took a strike, and she seemed to be going down. But she made contact on the next pitch and sent a slow grounder to Cindy, at first. Cindy had no chance to get Tobias. But she stepped on first to get Hobart, and now the Scrappers needed only one out.

But the tying run was at second. A mistake or two could end the season.

Tracy kept breathing deeply. She looked at

Gloria, who was holding up two fingers and yelling, "This is it. Two away. Stay alert."

All the people in the bleachers were standing now, going crazy. The Mustangs were yelling to the Hot Rods to keep the inning going. The Scrappers' fans were screaming for one more out.

Depola was up. He fouled off the first pitch and then took a low one for a ball. The next pitch was a ball of fire, and he swung a little late, but he sent a hard grounder scooting to Tracy's left.

Tracy broke for the ball, which was heading into right field. Cindy had cut to her right, but the ball skipped past her. Tracy's only chance was to dive. She left her feet, stretched all the way out, and felt the ball pound into her glove. At the same time, she felt an explosion of pain through her shoulder.

But she was thinking about Depola and his speed. She rolled over and—still on the ground—flipped the ball toward first base. Adam was running hard to cover the bag, and he was right where he was supposed to be. He caught the throw and stepped on the bag, just in front of Depola.

"Out!" the umpire howled, and the game was over.

Tracy heard the good news and felt the relief. She rolled off her shoulder and took a deep breath. The pain was worse now that she had time to think about it, but she was about to get up when Wanda got to her. "Are you all right?" Wanda asked her.

By then Cindy and Gloria and Adam were all there, and the rest of the team was gathering. Tracy was afraid someone was going to jump on top of her. She struggled to her feet, with Wanda's help. But she was clinging to her arm, holding it still, and she was bending forward. Around her, everyone was silent.

The Scrappers had just gotten their biggest win of the year, and no one was celebrating. They were all too worried about Tracy. "Hey," she said, "it's just a bruise. I'm okay."

"We need you when we play the Mustangs," Thurlow said.

"Don't worry. I'll be ready to go."

And that did set off some cheers. "We're going to get the Mustangs this time," Wilson yelled. "We're not dead yet."

Gloria had her arm around Tracy's shoulder. "Let's get you home," she said. "You need to get some ice on that shoulder."

But Tracy's parents had gotten there now. "This stupid game," Mrs. Matlock mumbled, as she took hold of Tracy. But Tracy's dad got in front of her and looked in her face. He seemed proud enough to burst. "What a *play* that was, Trace," he said. "You were *terrific* tonight."

"I can't believe how good you are." Tracy looked up to see that it was Maria speaking to her.

"I got lucky on that last play," Tracy said. "I just dove, and the ball stuck. And then I threw it where Adam was supposed to be—before I could even see him. And he was there."

She looked at Adam, who was grinning. "You saved us," he said.

"Hey, we'll come home with you," Heather said. "We'll help you ice that bruise."

"Yes. That would be so nice of you girls," Mrs. Matlock said.

"But she needs some rest," Gloria said.

"Yes, we do need to get you home, honey," Mrs. Matlock said. She was pulling Tracy away. "This may have been your last baseball game *ever*."

"Not a chance, Mom," Tracy said. "We've got to beat the Mustangs—twice! And that's just this season. Next year we could be *great*."

She smiled at Gloria, and Gloria flashed her a big thumbs-up.

And then Tracy finally noticed that the coach was standing nearby, waiting for his own turn. He stepped closer and then whispered in Tracy's ear, "I left you in because I knew you'd come through. Now that fear is gone, isn't it?"

"Yeah, it is. Thanks, Coach."

"Rest up. We need you next week, against the Mustangs."

"Don't worry. I'll be ready to go."

"Honey, you don't know that. We'll have to see," Mrs. Matlock said.

But Tracy had no fear at all.

TIPS FOR PLAYING SECOND BASE

1. As a second baseman you need good hands and quick feet. Be ready to cover a lot of ground and make throws from every angle. You may not need a cannon for an arm, but you need a rifle, strong and accurate.
2. You must learn to work well with the shortstop. You share the responsibility of covering second base. But remember, you also cover first when the first baseman handles a ground ball. So be ready to move, whenever the ball is hit.
3. When a runner attempts to steal second, you and the shortstop must know who is covering the bag. Talk it over or signal each other, but be sure you both know.
4. When you cover second on a double-play ball, get to the bag quickly and make a good target. As you catch the ball, drag your left foot across the bag, plant your right foot, then throw to first. This "pivot" is your toughest play. Practice it until it feels natural.
5. Field a sharply hit ground ball, get set, and then make a firm throw to first. But you will also handle slow rollers, balls hit to your right or left, over your head—or who knows where. Learn to throw the ball quickly from every body position.
6. On a ground ball hit up the middle, go after it, but let the shortstop cut inside and take the ball, if possible. The shortstop has a much easier throw to first.
7. Let the outfielders take all pop-ups that they can get to. Run to the ball, but when you hear the outfielder call you off, get out of the way.

8. On a pop-up behind first, take it if you can. You have a better angle than the first baseman does.

9. When you cover second, hurry to the bag and straddle it. Stand so you are facing at an angle that makes it easy to catch the ball and then put down the tag without having to adjust your feet.

10. When you tag a runner, place the ball between the bag and the runner and let the runner's foot slide into your glove. Use both hands for the tag, if you can, and then pull your hand away as soon as you feel the touch.

SOME RULES FROM COACH CARLTON

HITTING:

Don't try to smash the ball. Swing level and concentrate on "meeting" the ball. If you get good wood (or aluminum) on the ball, don't worry; it will go far enough.

BASE RUNNING:

When you're on base and the ball is hit in the air to an outfielder, your coach may tell you to "tag up." Go back to the bag and get ready. If the outfielder catches the ball, you may have a chance to advance to the next base after the catch. If the coach gives you the green light, take off—and go hard!

BEING A TEAM PLAYER:

Don't lose your temper with anyone—including yourself. No one likes to be around a player who throws bats or batting helmets, screams and swears, or otherwise acts like a jerk. Always be sure to show respect for everyone, including yourself.

ON DECK: THURLOW COATES, RIGHT FIELD.
DON'T MISS HIS STORY IN SCRAPPERS #9: *GRAND SLAM.*

Wilson was stepping to the plate now. Thurlow hoped the big guy would get on base somehow. Thurlow wanted to unload on one—the more runners on base the better.

But Wilson must have been watching Robbie. He got a high pitch and took a blind cut at it. And he popped the ball up, too. This one drifted toward Alan Pingree, the first baseman. Pingree shaded his eyes from the sun, trotted toward the mound, and hauled it in.

Two out, and now it was up to Thurlow.

As he walked to the plate, the Scrappers were whooping it up. "Look out, Mustangs," Chad Corrigan yelled. "Thurlow's going yard on you guys."

Wanda Coates, the first base coach—and Thurlow's mother—was clapping her hands. "Come on, son. Just meet the ball," she yelled. Mrs. Coates was a big woman, tall and red-haired. She could make enough noise to be heard over any crowd.

But Thurlow didn't like that—especially his mom calling him "son" in front of everyone. He and his mother had battled this summer after she pressured him to play on this team. The two of them had ironed some things out lately, but that still didn't mean that he liked having his mother out there on the field with him.

What Thurlow did like was the noise coming from the Mustangs. They were shouting, "Thurlow can't hit you, Justin. Don't worry about him."

But that's not what they were really thinking and Thurlow knew it. They knew Thurlow was the *man,* the guy they had to get out—or pitch around—if they were going to beat the Scrappers.

Lou's first pitch was up high, like so many he had already thrown today. The guy was trying to finish off the season, blow the Scrappers away, but he was forcing the ball too much, and it was getting away from him.

Thurlow didn't care. What he liked was that Lou wasn't tossing outside pitches, trying to get

Thurlow to nibble at something off the plate. He was coming after him, and that's just what Thurlow wanted.

The next pitch was even with Thurlow's shoulders, and it was all he could do to lay off. But now he was ahead in the count, 2 and 0, and in good shape.

He adjusted his helmet and then got set—coiled, ready. Early in the season, he hadn't cared one way or the other what happened to the Scrappers; he had stood at the plate like a guy hanging out on a corner. Now he was serious, and he wanted the Mustangs to know it.

Lou let another one fly—a burner—and this time it was in the strike zone. Thurlow's bat jumped to the ball, met it clean, and the ball took off like a launched rocket.

Thurlow dropped his bat, turned toward left field, and watched. It was a monster shot over the fence. He lost sight of it as it dropped beyond some trees, halfway across the park.

By then he had begun his trot. He didn't show off. He simply jogged around the bases.

He looked at no one, didn't acknowledge the wild cheers from his bench or from the crowd.

He did smile just a little when he saw Flowers standing at home plate with his hands on his hips. But he didn't say anything. He just stepped on the plate, slapped hands with Jeremy, and ran toward the dugout. As he did, the coach walked over to meet him. "What a blow," the coach said. "That was a perfect swing you took."

"Thanks," Thurlow said.

"The other players wanted to run out to home plate, but I stopped them. I told them not to show up the Mustangs this early in the game. No use making them mad." He grinned.

"That's right," Thurlow said. But the players were certainly ready for him when he reached the dugout. Everyone took turns slapping hands with him, telling him how great he was. And they looked a lot more confident now.

But Gloria got a good pitch and swung way too hard at it. She bounced it straight to the mound. Lou threw her out, and the inning was over.

Maybe Thurlow *was* going to have to win this game by himself today.